Birthday Mice!

Birthday Mice!

BY BETHANY ROBERTS

ILLUSTRATED BY DOUG CUSHMAN

Green Light Readers
HOUGHTON MIFFLIN HARCOURT
Boston   New York

First Green Light Readers edition, 2015

All rights reserved. Originally published in hardcover in the United States by
Clarion Books, an imprint of Houghton Mifflin Harcourt Publishing Company,
2002.

Green Light Readers™ and its logo are trademarks of HMH publishers LLC,
registered in the United States and other countries.

For information about permission to reproduce selections from this book,
write to Permissions, Houghton Mifflin Harcourt Publishing Company,
215 Park Avenue South, New York, New York 10003.

www.hmhco.com

The Library of Congress has cataloged the hardcover edition as follows:
Roberts, Bethany.
Birthday mice!/by Bethany Roberts; illustrated by Doug Cushman
p. cm.
Summary: A little mouse's very lively birthday party has the cowboy theme
he hoped for.
[1. Birthdays—Fiction. 2. Parties—Fiction. 3. Cowboys—Fiction. 4. Mice—
Fiction. 5. Animals—Fiction. 6. Stories in rhyme.] I. Cushman, Doug, ill.
II. Title.
PZ8.3.R5295 Bi2002
[E] 21
2001047594

ISBN: 978-0-544-45606-8 GLR paperback
ISBN: 978-0-544-45605-1 GLR paper over board

Manufactured in China
SCP 10 9 8 7 6 5 4 3 2 1

4500512346

Happy birthday, Cowboy Adam
and Cowboy Zach!
—B.R.

To Jennifer Greene, who waited
ages for this birthday party
—D.C.

Birthday mice
get ready for a party.

One little mouse
is two, two, two!

Balloons, balloons,
blow them up.

Red, yellow,
and blue, blue, blue!

Yippee-yi-yo!
Yippee-yi-yay!

A birthday cowboy.
Clippity-clop!

Howdy, cowboy!

Whoa! Watch out!

Oh, no!

POP! POP! POP!

The guests are coming.
Party time!

Here come the squirrels,
the rabbits too.

Cowboy boots that
stomp, stomp, stomp!

The chipmunks bring
a rope lasso.

Skunk gives spurs
that jingle, jangle.

Perfect for a
buckaroo!

Now let's play!
Sing cowboy songs!

Cowboy dancing,
do-si-do!

Wrangler whoops
and cowhand hollers!

Swing your partner
round and . . .

. . . OH!

The cake is smashed,
balloons are popped.

The party is
a mess, mess, mess!

Blow more balloons! And for the cake—
cowboy vittles. Yes, yes, yes!

Blow out the candles!
Wish, wish, wish!

I wish . . .
for a horse.

A horse?
Of course!

But how?
But how?

Magic, presto!
Zappity-zorse!

Yippee-yi-yo!
Yippee-yi-yay!
A horse for a mouse
to gallop away!